Magic, Myth, and Myst

GRIFFINS

DO YOU BELIEVE?

This series features creatures that excite our minds. They're magical. They're mythical. They're mysterious. They're also not real. They live in our stories. They're brought to life by our imaginations. Facts about these creatures are based on folklore, legends, and beliefs. We have a rich history of believing in the impossible. But these creatures only live in fantasies and dreams. Monsters do not live under our beds. They live in our heads!

45th Parallel Press

Published in the United States of America by Cherry Lake Publishing
Ann Arbor, Michigan
www.cherrylakepublishing.com

Reading Adviser: Marla Conn MS, Ed., Literacy specialist, Read-Ability, Inc.
Cover Design: Felicia Macheske

Photo Credits: © Eric Isselee/Shutterstock.com, cover; © withGod/Shutterstock.com, cover, 1; © garanga/Shutterstock.com, 5; © Erik Mandre/Shutterstock.com, 7; © TheWorst/Shutterstock.com, 8; © Suha Derbent/Shutterstock.com, 11; © Ralf Juergen Kraft/Shutterstock.com, 12; © Nejron Photo/Shutterstock.com, 15; © DOMENICA13/Shutterstock.com, 17; © real-ultramarin/Shutterstock.com, 18; © Akvaartist/Shutterstock.com, 21; © Sarunyu L/Shutterstock.com, 22; © Dieter Hawlan/Shutterstock.com, 24; © Anton V. Tokarev/Shutterstock.com, 27; © Vuk Kostic/Shutterstock.com, 29

Graphic Elements Throughout: © denniro/Shutterstock.com; © Libellule/Shutterstock.com; © sociologas/Shutterstock.com; © paprika/Shutterstock.com; © ilolab/Shutterstock.com; © Bruce Rolff/Shutterstock.com

45th Parallel Press is an imprint of Cherry Lake Publishing.

Library of Congress Cataloging-in-Publication Data has been filed and is available at catalog.loc.gov

Cherry Lake Publishing would like to acknowledge the work of The Partnership for 21st Century Skills. Please visit *www.p21.org* for more information.

Printed in the United States of America
Corporate Graphics

TABLE of CONTENTS

Chapter One

A Monster Mix

What are griffins? What do they look like? What's their job? How do they have babies?

"All hail the king of creatures." Griffins are a **hybrid**. Hybrids are combinations. Griffins are part-lion. Lions are the kings of beasts. Griffins are part-eagle. Eagles are the kings of birds. Griffins rule the land. They rule the skies. They're noble. They're powerful.

Griffins have a lion's body. They have a lion's tail. They have a lion's ears. They have an eagle's head. They have an eagle's chest. They have an eagle's wings. They have an eagle's sharp claws. Their bodies are tan like a lion. Their wings and feathers are white or blue.

Some griffins have a snake's tail.

Explained by Science!

Not all animals can be crossbred. Crossbred means combined. For example, pigs and monkeys can't mate. They can't have babies. Animals must belong to the same general group. They must have the same number of chromosomes. Chromosomes carry information about genes. Genes determine traits. Offspring of crossbred animals have traits from both parents. Offspring are children. Ligers are hybrids. They're the children of male lions and female tigers. They have a lion's full mane. They have a tiger's stripes. Hybrid animals can't have children. Hybrid animals are interesting. But some scientists think it's a bad idea to mix animals. Hybrid animals don't live long. They have more health problems.

Like eagles, griffins have a large wingspan.

Griffins have fire in their eyes. They are big. One claw is the size of a cow's horn. Griffins have a **flexible** spine. Flexible means able to bend. They can move easily. Their back claws are long. They're sharp. They can **retract**. This means they can be pulled in and out. Their tail is strong. It can move. It can grab things. It's like a **rudder**. It steers. It helps griffins move quickly. Griffins' feathers are shiny and smooth. They're waterproof. Griffins have sharp beaks.

They're made to hunt. They eat anything. They eat mice. They eat young dragons. They eat horses. They eat humans.

Griffins live in the skies. They live in the mountains. They find gold. Treasure hunters look for gold. Griffins became guards. They protect their gold. They're mean. They're tough. They fight hard. They eat hunters. They're known as **guardians** of treasure. Guardians are protectors.

Griffins mate for life. If their partner died, griffins would live alone. Female griffins fly around. They look for caves. Their cave has to have lots of room. They have small entrances. This protects eggs from the weather. Female griffins build a nest. They use gold. They lay eggs. They protect their eggs. They protect the nests.

Griffins are similar to dragons.

Chapter Two

A Powerful Combination

What powers do griffins have? How are they like lions? How are they like eagles? What's magical about their claws?

Griffins have the powers of lions and eagles. They fly like eagles. They fly high. They fly anywhere. They fly as fast as eagles.

They see very well. They have an eagle's vision. **Vision** is the ability to see. They see things from far away. While flying, they see mice running in fields. They hear well. They hear animals moving underground.

They're strong. They're brave. They have a lion's power. They have a lion's muscles. Their long legs push them forward. They can move at high speed.

Griffins have all the strength of a lion.

Griffins are stronger than eight lions. They're stronger than a hundred eagles. They can deal with any type of weather. Storms don't bother them. They **adapt** to their environments. Adapt means they can change. Griffins can get used to any setting. They live a long time. Most live about 800 years.

Griffins are wise. They have a lot of tricks. They make up riddles. They make up games. They trick people. They give people **challenges**. Challenges are hard contests. People who win get to live. Losers get eaten.

There aren't many griffins in the world.

When Fantasy Meets Reality!

Ruppell's griffon vultures live in Africa. They're large. Their wings are 8 feet (2.5 meters) long. They're the world's highest flying birds. They fly over 36,000 feet (10.9 kilometers) above sea level. One griffon vulture got sucked into a plane engine. The plane was flying 36,100 feet (11 km) high. Griffon vultures have special cells. This lets them fly in low air pressure. This lets them fly with less oxygen. Griffon vultures fly long distances. They fly over 90 miles (145 km). They fly about 22 miles (35.4 km) per hour. They fly for 6 to 7 hours a day. They fly to make nests. They fly to eat. They eat dead animals. They insert their heads under the skin. They get into the dead animals' bodies. They like rotten meat.

Kings were afraid enemies would try to poison them.

Griffins have powerful claws. Their claws can kill. They rip meat apart. They grab prey. They help lift prey into the sky.

Their claws are also magical. They change color. This happens when there's poison around. People wanted griffin claws to help test for poison. They put griffin claws in their drinks. Some people made cups out of griffins' claws. They waited to see if the claws changed color. Griffin claws protected people from death. They protected people from sickness.

Griffins also have magical feathers. Their feathers cure **blindness**. Blindness is not being able to see.

Chapter Three

Slaying the Beast

What are ways to kill griffins? What are griffins' enemies?

It's hard to get griffin claws and feathers. People have to find griffins. They have to win them over. This rarely happens. But some holy men have been successful. This happened in the Middle Ages. These holy men healed griffins. They helped them. Griffins were thankful. They returned the kindness. They gave the men their claws and feathers.

Griffins are good fighters. They're good hunters. They're fierce. They attack to kill. They don't fight fair. Since they can fly, people can't keep up. People can't trap griffins. Griffins can escape easily. It's hard to kill griffins.

A griffin can give its feathers to humans as a gifts.

It would be hard to get griffins to stay in one place.

Griffins can be **beheaded**. Beheaded means chopping off the head. Griffins can't grow new heads. So, they would die. They can die from **drowning**. Griffins can't breathe underwater. They'd choke to death. They can also die from burning. Griffins can't live through fire. They'd choke from the smoke. They'd turn to ashes.

Griffins can die from a **fatal** wound. Fatal means deadly. Some people fight with weapons. These weapons can cut griffins. Griffins hate **basilisks**. Basilisks are monsters. They're the king of snakes. They're enemies of griffins. Griffins and basilisks fight. Basilisks can cut griffins. They can kill griffins.

SURVIVAL TIPS!

- Stay away from mountains. Stay away from caves. Griffins could live there.
- Learn how to fly. Learn how to skydive. You have to be able to fight in the air.
- Trap griffins. Drug them. Get them to stay in one place. Tie up their wings. Tie up their legs.
- Get a sharp sword. Fight with the sword. Behead griffins.
- Trap griffins underwater. Drown them.
- Trap griffins in a building. Set the building on fire.
- Study a lot. Outwit griffins. Accept one of their challenges. Win by being smarter than them. Remember to think outside the box.

Chapter Four

From Dinosaur Bones to Legends

How long have griffins been around? What did Adrienne Mayor discover?

Griffins have been around since ancient times. Herodotus was an ancient Greek **historian**. Historians study history. Herodotus traveled around the world. He met a lot of people. He visited new places. He took notes on everything. He met Scythians. Scythia was the area around central Asia and Ukraine. Scythians hunted for gold. They told Herodotus about griffins. They said they fought griffins for gold. They shared details about what griffins ate. They shared details about how griffins made nests. They shared details about where griffins lived. They found griffins around the Gobi Desert. The Gobi Desert is in China and Mongolia. This area had lots of gold.

Griffins stand for loyalty, power, and honor.

Adrienne Mayor is a historian. She is a **folklore** expert. Folklore is stories. She studies griffins. She thinks griffins started with **traders**. Traders are people who trade things. Traders traveled long distances. They traveled across the Gobi Desert. They traveled from Europe to Mongolia.

There were white **fossils** in this area. Fossils are the remains of plants and animals. This area was where Scythians hunted for gold.

The fossils were from the Protoceratops. Protoceratops were dinosaurs. They were the size of a wolf. They had animal ears. They had four legs. They had a bird beak. They had long bird shoulders.

Fossils like this might have inspired stories about griffins.

Know the Lingo!

- **Alce:** another name for griffin
- **Aquiline:** like an eagle
- **Centaur:** monster with a human's body on a horse's body
- **Chimera:** monster with a lion's head, goat's body, and snake's tail
- **Cockatrice:** monster with a dragon's tail and chicken parts
- **Harpy:** monster with a female body and a bird's wings and claws
- **Hippogriff:** monster child of griffins and horses
- **Keythong:** another name for griffin
- **Leonine:** looking like a lion
- **Opinicus:** monster with a griffin's head, lion's body, and camel's tail
- **Satyr:** monster with a goat's legs, ears, horns, and tail
- **Sphinx:** monster with a lion's body and a human head
- **Talon:** hooked, sharp claw of a bird of prey
- **Ziz:** giant griffin-like bird in Jewish myths

There were other fossils. Big claws were found. These claws were from different dinosaurs. All these fossils made people think. They sparked people's imaginations. They inspired stories about griffins. Traders saw these fossils. They made up stories. They shared these stories with others. Griffins became popular.

Some experts think griffin stories started in India. Indians loved griffins. They thought griffins were good at finding gold. They thought griffins used their beaks to mine gold. They thought griffins guarded their gold. They thought griffins built nests near gold.

Many monsters may have been inspired by real animals.

Chapter Five

Gods and Warriors

What are some stories with griffins?
What happened with the Arimaspians?

Some people believe the Greek gods created griffins. The gods wanted a powerful animal. They wanted the animal to work for them.

Ancient Greeks had stories about griffins. Apollo was a god. He was the god of fire and sun. He had a **chariot**. A chariot is a cart with wheels. Griffins pulled Apollo's chariot. They pulled him from the sun to the earth.

Griffins fought against Amazons. Amazons were beautiful women. They were fierce. They were warriors. People think this war was about light fighting dark.

Griffins are a popular symbol.

Real-World Connection

Some U.S. scientists are growing human organs inside animals. They're using sheep and pigs. They want to give the organs to people. They're calling these organs *chimeras.* Scientists inject human stem cells inside animal eggs. Then, they inject eggs into pigs or sheep. The organs grow inside the animals. The scientists would take the organs out. They'd put the organs into humans who need them. Some people have to wait years for an organ donation. These chimeras could save lives. But some people don't like this idea. They don't agree with hybrids. They don't agree with combining humans and animals. Pablo Ross is a scientist. He said, "We're not trying to make a chimera just because we want to see some kind of monstrous creature." He wants to "improve peoples' lives."

Griffins fought against Arimaspians. Arimaspians lived near Scythia. They lived at the bottom of the mountains. They were men. They had only one eye. They were big. They had blonde hair. They were mean. They were known to eat humans. They rode horses. They were really good at riding horses.

They were at war with griffins. They fought for a long time. They tried to steal griffins' gold. They used their horses. They attacked on horseback. This is why griffins hated horses. Griffins killed the Arimaspians. They ate the men. They ate the horses.

Fighting griffins isn't a good idea.

Did You Know?

There are 24 ways to spell *griffin*. These are the other spellings: gryffen, girphinne, greffon, grefyne, grephoun, griffen, griffion, griffon, griffoun, griffown, griffun, griffyn, grifon, grifyn, griphin, griphon, gryffin, gryffon, gryfon, gryfoun, gryphen, gryphin, and gryphon.

Griffin might come from the Greek word grypos. This means "curved."

The griffin is the symbol of the Philadelphia Museum of Art. The griffins sit on the corners of the museum's roof. They protect the art. They are made of bronze.

Griffins store what they don't eat. They keep leftover meat. They hang it from trees. They bury it underground. They eat it later.

Griffins guarded the Holy Grail. The Holy Grail caught the blood of Jesus Christ. It's special. It's believed to give people powers. Some people think it gives immortality. Immortality is the ability to live forever.

People have sold antelope horns as griffin claws. They've sold ostrich eggs as griffin eggs. They've tricked people. They sold these things for a lot of money.

Pictures of griffins are on tombs. Tombs are places where people are buried. Griffins guard people. They guard people in life and death.

Some people believe griffins were the "hounds of Zeus." Zeus was the king of the Greek gods.

Consider This!

Take a Position: Reread Chapter 4. Read *The Griffin and the Dinosaur: How Adrienne Mayor Discovered a Fascinating Link Between Myth and Science*. This book studies the connection between the legend of the griffin and dinosaurs. Do you think griffins may have really existed? Argue your point with reasons and evidence.

Say What? Research other monsters from Greek myths. Explain which monster is most like griffins. Explain how they're alike. Explain how they're different. Explain which monster you like best.

Think About It! Griffins are a hybrid. Create your own hybrid monster. Research different animals. Identify the animal parts. Identify the animal behaviors. Explain your thinking.

Learn More

- Aronson, Marc, with Adrienne Mayor and Chris Muller (illustrator). *The Griffin and the Dinosaur: How Adrienne Mayor Discovered a Fascinating Link Between Myth and Science*. Washington, DC: National Geographic, 2014.
- Marsico, Katie. *Beastly Monsters: From Dragons to Griffins*. Minneapolis: Lerner Publications, 2017.
- Sautter, A. J. *A Field Guide to Griffins, Unicorns, and Other Mythical Beasts*. North Mankato, MN: Capstone Press, 2015.

Glossary

adapt (uh-DAPT) to go with the flow; to change

basilisk (BAS-ih-lisk) snake monster that is the king of snakes

beheaded (bih-HED-id) chopped off the head

blindness (BLINDE-nes BLINDE-nes) losing the ability to see

challenges (CHAL-inj-ez) contests; difficult tasks

chariot (CHAR-ee-uht) two-wheeled cart pulled by strong animals

drowning (DROUN-ing) being unable to breath underwater

fatal (FAY-tuhl) deadly

flexible (FLEK-suh-buhl) being able to bend, having the ability to move or change easily

folklore (FOHK-lor) stories from cultures usually shared orally

fossils (FAH-suhlz) preserved remains or impressions of plants and animals

guardians (GAHR-dee-uhnz) protectors

historian (his-TOR-ee-uhn) person who studies and records history

hybrid (HYE-brid) a thing made by combining two different things; the offspring or children of two different animals

retract (rih-TRAKT) to pull in or out

rudder (RUHD-ur) steer

traders (TRAY-durz) people who trade goods for money or other goods

vision (VIZH-uhn) ability to see

Index

About the Author

Dr. Virginia Loh-Hagan is an author, university professor, former classroom teacher, and curriculum designer. She thinks her dog, Woody, is a mix of dog, goat, cat, and dragon. She lives in San Diego with her very tall husband and very naughty dogs. To learn more about her, visit www.virginialoh.com.